Catherine the Great

and Her Teatime Tagalongs

Catherine the Great

and Her Teatime Tagalongs

By Karen Swensen

Illustrated by Kelly Kirkman

PELICAN PUBLISHING COMPANY
GRETNA 2005

For the great Catherines in my life: my mother and daughter.
And for John and Kimmy and especially St. Jude.

The word "Pelican" and the depiction of a pelican are trademarks
of Pelican Publishing Company, Inc., and are registered in the
U.S. Patent and Trademark Office.

Library of Congress Cataloging-in-Publication Data

Swensen, Karen.
  Catherine the Great and her teatime tagalongs / by Karen Swensen ; illustrated by Kelly Kirkman.
    p. cm.
  Summary: Catherine is an only child, but her toys keep her company even though they do not behave as perfectly as they might.
  ISBN-13: 978-1-58980-343-5 (alk. paper)
  ISBN-10: 1-58980-343-4 (alk. paper)
  [1. Toys—Fiction. 2. Stories in rhyme.] I. Kirkman, Kelly, ill. II. Title.
  PZ8.3.S99555Cat 2005
  [E]—dc22

                        2005012934

Printed in Singapore
Published by Pelican Publishing Company, Inc.
1000 Burmaster Street, Gretna, Louisiana 70053

In a land full of toys that's far, far away, lives a
bright little girl who loves to play. She's Catherine
the Great, spelled with a "C," a sweet, smiling
cherub as cute as can be, from her round, rosy
cheeks to her chubby, pink toes, from the curls on
her head to her small, button nose.

But it's her eyes that sparkle and sing and dance and say so much with only a glance. And that's not all. They can read and see . . . all the goodness in everything. She is the key!

And even though Catherine is an only child at home, she never gets bored since she's never alone.

There's Baby Doll and Lamb and Eddie Elephant.
It's true! Big Bear, Bonnie Bunny, and Lady
Ladybug, too! And while the whole day is fun, the
best time of all is just after lunch but before evening
falls. At three o'clock sharp, Catherine sets out for
tea and the tagalongs climb to her house in the tree.

The table is set with the finest of care, with six tiny chairs and a big one for Bear. He is the biggest, by far, of them all. In fact, everyone else is really quite small.

"C'mon with the tea and the crumpets already!"
he shouts to Catherine as she holds the pot steady.
But Catherine won't rush and pays him no mind
'cause she knows in his heart Bear is really quite
kind. He's just in a rush and can't stand to wait,
even when no one around him is late.

"Be patient, Big Bear," Catherine says with a grin. And Bear takes the deep breath that will relax him. And while others just think that Bear's big, loud, and tall, it's Catherine who sees he's the softest of all. So it doesn't surprise her when the others just stare as Bear helps Lady Ladybug pull out her pink chair.

"This way, young lady . . . come, come take a seat. Let's drink our fine tea and share something to eat."

Now Lady Ladybug is, shall we say, a girl's girl, from her polka-dot purse to her lashes that curl. "Yes, yes, Mr. Bear, I should like that a lot, but I won't share my treat; no I won't. I will not. I should like my own tea and my own little scone. And I don't want to share. Please leave me alone!"

How selfish Lady Ladybug often could be, but there was much more inside her that Catherine could see. Lady Ladybug never wanted to share because she never knew anyone really to care. If Catherine could just convince her she's wrong, she'd learn how she's loved by all tagalongs.

"Lady Ladybug don't you know how your friends like you near? How they huddle so close and lean in just to hear? The stories you imagine and tell to yourself are better, I'm sure, than any book on the shelf."

And with that, Lady Ladybug looked at the toys and confidently told them the story of Joy. Joy laughed a faint laugh, "Yeah, this one's for me," as she peered from behind a branch on the tree. The little lamb was outside, too shy to come in, so she strained to hear about the race she would win.

Lady Ladybug whispered, "It was close to a tie, but the lamb ate still faster, pie after pie." It was a silly, short story that made everyone laugh about a pie-eating contest 'tween Joy and a calf!

And when it was over, Joy came in from the heat to join her new friends and take her own seat. And Catherine was glad to share her fun tea with the lamb whom she knew was the sweetest of sweet. And right then, right there, Joy settled her sights on the big, goofy elephant taking big bites.

He's clumsy and messy and spills on the floor big crumbly crumbs, and oh, so much more. Eddie Elephant slurps and burps at the tea! Then he stops, blinks, and braces himself for a sneeze. . .

"ACHOOOO!" he yells as the plates start to quake. Oh no! What a mess he's going to make! The table is shaking, the teacups in air, and all they could do was just sit there and stare.

When the sneeze finally died and the air finally cleared, the tagalongs saw 'twas as bad as they feared. The scones and the crumpets were all on the floor and the teapot had flown right out of the door! The cups and the saucers had crashed to the ground, and the spoons and the forks lay in a big mound. The napkins were littered all over the place and the tablecloth landed on Big Bear's shocked face!

"I'm trapped! I can't see! Your sneeze has confused
me!" yelled Bear to the elephant who said only,
"'Scuse me."

"Get this thing off me! What's taking so long?"
said a very mad Bear whose patience was gone.

"I'm sorry for you, my dear friend, Big Bear," said Joy very softly. "Bet it's dark under there. But please don't be mad at Elephant, please! He couldn't help that he had to sneeze."

Big Bear thought about this and then thought some more . . . and then unleashed a very loud roar.

"Hee! Hee!" He was laughing—laughing
so hard that his laughs could be heard way
down in the yard. Then all chimed in, they
were laughing with glee. How much more
fun could this tea really be?

And all of the while, Catherine just watched, not
caring a bit that her teatime was botched.

'Cause Catherine knew—knew all along—that the sneeze was no sneeze. No, they had it all wrong! Eddie Elephant was neither clumsy nor sneezy. He just liked to make laughs for to him it was pleasing.

So she shot him a glance with a knowing, sweet eye, when all of a sudden, Bonnie Bunny hopped by.

Hop! Thump! Hop! Thump! She bounced through the room. Hop! Hop! Uh-oh! Bonnie Bunny went "boom"! She fell to the floor but bounced right back up and at the same time scooped up a teacup. She jumped and she thumped and she soared through the air. "Hi! High! Hi! High! Hi! High!" said the hare.

But that was the only word she would speak, and no one knew what she really did mean. Did "hi" mean "hello" or did "high" mean "up there"? No one knew except for the hare. Still Bonnie just smiled, never missing a beat, reaching out her teacup from her usual seat.

"Hello? Can't you see that there's no tea to serve?" Lady Ladybug sneered, "Well, you've got some nerve! You've scooped up *my* cup and since there's no tea, I'll thank you so kindly to return my cup, please."

But Bonnie Bunny just smiled and shouted, "Hi! High!" And Catherine the Great winked her left eye.

You see, Catherine knew that her tagalong bunny
was as bright as the big, yellow sun was so sunny.
Bonnie Bunny was smart, maybe smarter than all.
"Hi! High! Hi! High!" Bonnie thumped up the wall.
And there it was on the very top shelf—a second tea
set. Bonnie found it herself!

So "hi" did mean "hello" and "high" did mean "up there." And everyone clapped, why, even Big Bear. He said, "Quick! Let's begin! Let's waste no more time."

"I agree," said Lady Ladybug pointing. "That one is mine." She picked out a saucer and so did shy Joy along with Eddie Elephant and the rest of the toys.

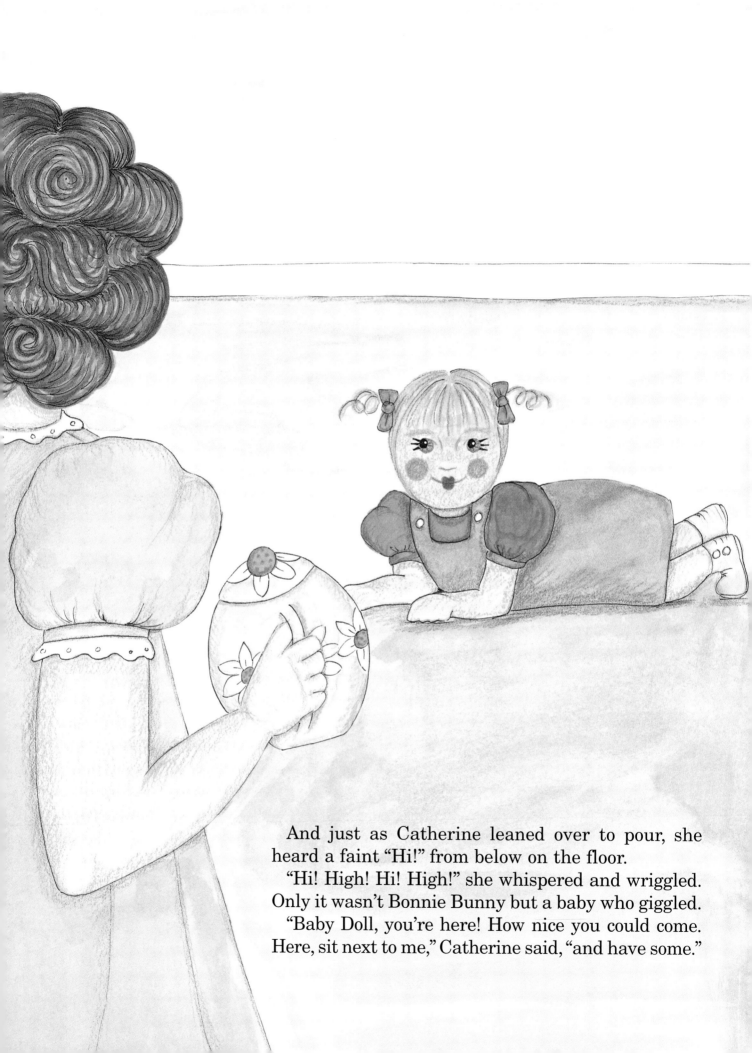

And just as Catherine leaned over to pour, she heard a faint "Hi!" from below on the floor.

"Hi! High! Hi! High!" she whispered and wriggled. Only it wasn't Bonnie Bunny but a baby who giggled.

"Baby Doll, you're here! How nice you could come. Here, sit next to me," Catherine said, "and have some."

"And have some! And have some!" Baby Doll
would repeat as all of the tagalongs got ready to eat.
"You must be hungry," said kind, little Joy.
"Hungry! Hungry!" said the baby doll toy.

And just then they noticed that Baby Doll copies everything that she hears and everything that she sees. And that's when they realized they'd better be good if Baby Doll was to grow up like a little girl should. And so Lady Ladybug offered to share, and Bear patiently waited as she climbed in her chair. And Joy sat beside her and made her feel loved, while Bonnie Bunny waved, "Hi! High!" from way up above.

And while Eddie Elephant made funny faces, Catherine the Great thought of faraway places. Her tagalongs aren't perfect, but each one is good, ready to take on adventures, she thought. Yes, they would.